Dear Parent:

Have Respect

This delightful tale is rich with opportunities for parent-child "heart-to-hearts." You'll read about Clifford and his doggy pals abandoning their eagerly anticipated play date in order to rescue—of all things—kittens in distress. Imagine Clifford, Cleo, and T-Bone giving up a chance for pure doggy fun in order to help members of what had been considered an alien species. The kittens, Billy and Betty, manage to win the dog pals' sympathy, probably because dogs and cats and everyone else understand how it feels to be small, helpless, and afraid. Any child can certainly relate to that.

For their good deeds, Clifford, Cleo, and T-Bone are rewarded with three newfound and very grateful friends: the kittens and their mom. What's more, the dog trio makes an important discovery—cats are not really the enemies of dogs once you get to know them. In fact, felines can turn out be wonderfully loyal friends. Reading about this offers an opportunity for you and your child to talk about dogs and cats that you both know who *do* get along, perhaps even your own. It then allows you to make the broader point: Those who may seem to be different can often become the best of friends.

In *Dogs and Cats,* it turns out that once the rescue is accomplished, the barriers vanish and there is joy all around. Both the dogs and the cats learn to trust each other despite their apparent differences. This story provides you with an opportunity to talk to your child about reconsidering distrust of anyone just because he or she seems different. In the end, this slice out of Clifford's life demonstrates the merits of respecting everyone. The bottom line is implicit advice to have an open mind and be respectful. Then, like Clifford and his dog pals, you too may enjoy the rewards of making new friends.

Adele M. Brodkin, Ph.D.

Visit Clifford at scholastic.com/clifford

ISBN 0-439-22460-8

Copyright © 2001 Scholastic Entertainment Inc. All rights reserved.
Based on the CLIFFORD THE BIG RED DOG book series published by Scholastic Inc. TM & © Norman Bridwell.
SCHOLASTIC, CARTWHEEL BOOKS, and associated logos are trademarks and/or registered trademarks
of Scholastic Inc. CLIFFORD, CLIFFORD THE BIG RED DOG, CLIFFORD & COMPANY,
and associated logos are trademarks and/or registered trademarks of Norman Bridwell.

Library of Congress Cataloging-in-Publication Data is available

10 9 8 7 6 5 4 3 2 1   01 02 03 04 05 06

Printed in the U.S.A.   24
First printing, November 2001

Clifford THE BIG RED DOG®

Dogs and Cats

Adapted by David L. Harrison

Illustrated by Josie Yee

**Based on the Scholastic book series
"Clifford The Big Red Dog"
by Norman Bridwell**

From the television script
"The Truth About Dogs and Cats"
by Bob Carrau

SCHOLASTIC INC.

New York   Toronto   London   Auckland   Sydney   Mexico City
New Delhi   Hong Kong

"Clifford and Cleo are coming soon,
And all we're going to do is play!
I can hardly wait to see my friends.
It's going to be a perfect day!"

"Hmm, did I just hear a noise?

It sounded like a *meow* to me.

I don't know what my friends will say

If a cat is hiding in my tree!"

"T-Bone! Hi! I'm ready to play!
Wow! Look at all those toys!"

"Hold it, fellas, what was that?
Was it a meowing noise?"

"Betty, where did Mama go?

What will happen to us now?"

"Billy, how do we get down?

Now we're stuck." *Meow! Meow!*

"Don't look now—but you have cats!
You shouldn't have them in your yard!"

"We climbed up here to look for Mom.
But getting down is really hard!"

"You know what I have always heard?
Dogs and cats don't get along!
We need to get those kittens down
And send them home where they belong."

"We can't get down without our mom!
We don't know where our mom can be."

"Poor little guys! They need their mom
So she can get them down the tree."

"You think that we could find their mom?
She must be somewhere in the city."

"How will we know which cat she is?"

"She's black and white and really pretty!"

"This sure is a big surprise!
I came to play with T-Bone's hat."

"And *I* came over for hide-and-seek—
But now we're seeking for a cat!"

"Every corner has a cat!
And half of them are black and white."

"We'll have to talk to lots of cats
Until we find the one that's right."

"Have you lost a pair of kittens?
We found them up in T-Bone's tree."

"One, two, three, four.
No, my kittens
are all with me."

"Me? I have no time for kids.
I serenade the moon all night.
I nap all day to get my rest.
Excuse me, please. You're in my light."

"You're black and white and really pretty.

Could *you* be our missing mom?"

"I would help you if I could.

Unfortunately, my name is Tom."

"This is tougher than I thought.
Finding Mom is really hard!"

"We have to get those kittens down!
Let's go back to T-Bone's yard."

Mew mew mew mew.

"Someone tell us what to do!"

Meow meow meow meow.

"We want down—but don't know how!"

"Cleo, I can't touch the limb.

See if you can reach up to it."

"Now you're getting very close!

One more doggy ought to do it!"

"Why is everyone looking at me?
I don't know how to climb that high!"

"Come on, T-Bone, sure you can!
Climb on Cleo's head and try!"

"Golly, T-Bone. You're so brave!
Wait until our mama hears!"

"I can't believe what I just saw!
Those dogs have saved my little dears!"

"Hooray! Your mom is here at last!
We looked for her all over town!"

"Mama! Come and meet our friends!
They're the ones who got us down!"

"Look at all of T-Bone's toys!
Wow! Let's play and have some fun!"

"Look at me in this old hat!
Let's have a party, everyone!"

"I've always heard that dogs and cats

Can never get along a bit.

But you've been friends to both my kids!"

"Come on! Let's play some tag!"

"You're it!"

"Hey! Somebody throw the ball!"

"Ha! Who turned the sprinkler on?"

"Ready or not, here I come!"

"I'll race you twice around the lawn!"

"Let's play a game of keep-away!"

"Cleo, Cleo, can't catch me!"

"See if you can jump this high!"

"Come play tug-of-war with me!"

"Guess what, T-Bone? We like you!
Playing tag with you is fun!"

"Thank you, kids! I like you, too!
Treats on me for everyone!"

"When we get to know each other,
Dogs and cats don't need to fuss."

"We couldn't say it any better!
Clifford speaks for all of us!"

BOOKS IN THIS SERIES:

Welcome to Birdwell Island: Everyone on Birdwell Island thinks that Clifford is just too big! But when there's an emergency, Clifford The Big Red Dog teaches everyone to have respect—even for those who are different.

A Puppy to Love: Emily Elizabeth's birthday wish comes true: She gets a puppy to love! And with her love and kindness, Clifford The Small Red Puppy becomes Clifford The Big Red Dog!

The Big Sleep Over: Clifford has to spend his first night without Emily Elizabeth. When he has trouble falling asleep, his Birdwell Island friends work together to make sure that he—and everyone else—gets a good night's sleep.

No Dogs Allowed: No dogs in Birdwell Island Park? That's what Mr. Bleakman says—before he realizes that sharing the park with dogs is much more fun.

An Itchy Day: Clifford has an itchy patch! He's afraid to go to the vet, so he tries to hide his scratching from Emily Elizabeth. But Clifford soon realizes that it's better to be truthful and trust the person he loves most— Emily Elizabeth.

The Doggy Detectives: Oh, no! Emily Elizabeth is accused of stealing Jetta's gold medal—and then her shiny mirror! But her dear Clifford never doubts her innocence and, with his fellow doggy detectives, finds the real thief.

Follow the Leader: While playing follow-the-leader with Clifford and T-Bone, Cleo learns that playing fair is the best way to play!

The Big Red Mess: Clifford tries to stay clean for the Dog of the Year contest, but he ends up becoming a big red mess! However, when Clifford helps the judge reach the shore safely, he finds that he doesn't need to stay clean to be the Dog of the Year.

The Big Surprise: Poor Clifford. It's his birthday, but none of his friends will play with him. Maybe it's because they're all busy. . . planning his surprise party!

The Wild Ice Cream Machine: Charley and Emily Elizabeth decide to work the ice cream machine themselves. Things go smoothly. . . until the lever gets stuck and they find themselves knee-deep in ice cream!

Dogs and Cats: Can dogs and cats be friends? Clifford, T-Bone, and Cleo don't think so. But they have a change of heart after they help two lost kittens find their mother.

The Magic Ball: Emily Elizabeth trusts Clifford to deliver a package to the post office, but he opens it and breaks the gift inside. Clifford tries to hide his blunder, but Emily Elizabeth appreciates honesty and understands that accidents happen.